JOHN CORIGLIANO

"HOW LIKE PELLUCID STATUES, DADDY. OR LIKE A . . . AN ENGINE."

ED-3973
First printing: October 1995

G. SCHIRMER, *Inc.*

DISTRIBUTED BY
HAL•LEONARD CORPORATION
7777 W. BLUEMOUND RD. P.O. BOX 13819 MILWAUKEE, WI 53213

Program Note

In reading John Ashbery's poem, "No Longer Very Clear," I was struck by the contrasting imagery in the adjacent phrases "How like pellucid statues, Daddy, Or like a . . . an engine." The frozen translucent statues seemed to me to be a marvelous foil for the pulsating hot energy of an engine—both images, as seen through the eyes of a child, readily evoked musical ideas.

The unique sound of double reeds seemed at once to be the right choice, and fulfilled a desire I have always had to write for multiple bassoons. The work utilizes row techniques, and is in two parts—the first a picture of the frozen pellucid statues, and the second, an aural portrait of the energy and acceleration inherent in the words "an engine."

—JOHN CORIGLIANO

No Longer Very Clear

It is true that I can no longer remember very well
the time when we first began to know each other.
However, I do remember very well
the first time we met. You walked in sunlight,
holding a daisy. You said, "Children make unreliable witnesses."

Now, so long after that time,
I keep the spirit of it throbbing still.
The ideas are still the same, and they expand
to fill vast, antique cubes.

My daughter was reading one just the other day.
She said, "How like pellucid statues, Daddy. Or like a . . . an engine."

In this house of blues the cold creeps stealthily upon us.
I do not dare to do what I fantasize doing.
With time the blue congeals into roomlike purple
that takes the shape of alcoves, landings . . .
Everything is like something else,
I should have waited before I learned this.

—JOHN ASHBERY

for WNYC

"HOW LIKE PELLUCID STATUES, DADDY OR LIKE A… AN ENGINE."

from *No Longer Very Clear*, by John Ashbery

John Corigliano
(1994)

* Repeat figures *ad lib.;* slowly shorten time between figures.

Tempo primo (♩ = ca. 50)
9
p legato
p legato
p legato
p legato
15
pp
pp
pp
pp
♩ = 60 (slightly faster)
21
push
forward
p
p
mp
mp

rall.
Tempo primo (♩ = ca. 50)
legato
♩ = 60 (slightly faster)
push forward
push forward
moving ahead steadily
♩ = ca. 72 – 80
A tempo primo
♩ = ca. 50

* *p*, *stacc. ad lib.* with large spaces between the notes (or note groups). Do not coordinate with others. *Slowly cresc.* and *accel.* after all are playing. As tempo becomes faster, *very gradually* line up with other players and make all notes even, so that at the end, all four players are synchronized.

rall.
Tempo primo (♩ = ca. 50)
p legato
pp
♩ = 60 (slightly faster)
p
push forward
push forward
moving ahead steadily
mf
f
♩ = ca. 72 – 80
ff
f
A tempo primo
♩ = ca. 50
ff
p

* *p*, *stacc. ad lib.* with large spaces between the notes (or note groups). Do not coordinate with others. *Slowly cresc.* and *accel.* after all are playing. As tempo becomes faster, *very gradually* line up with other players and make all notes even, so that at the end, all four players are synchronized.

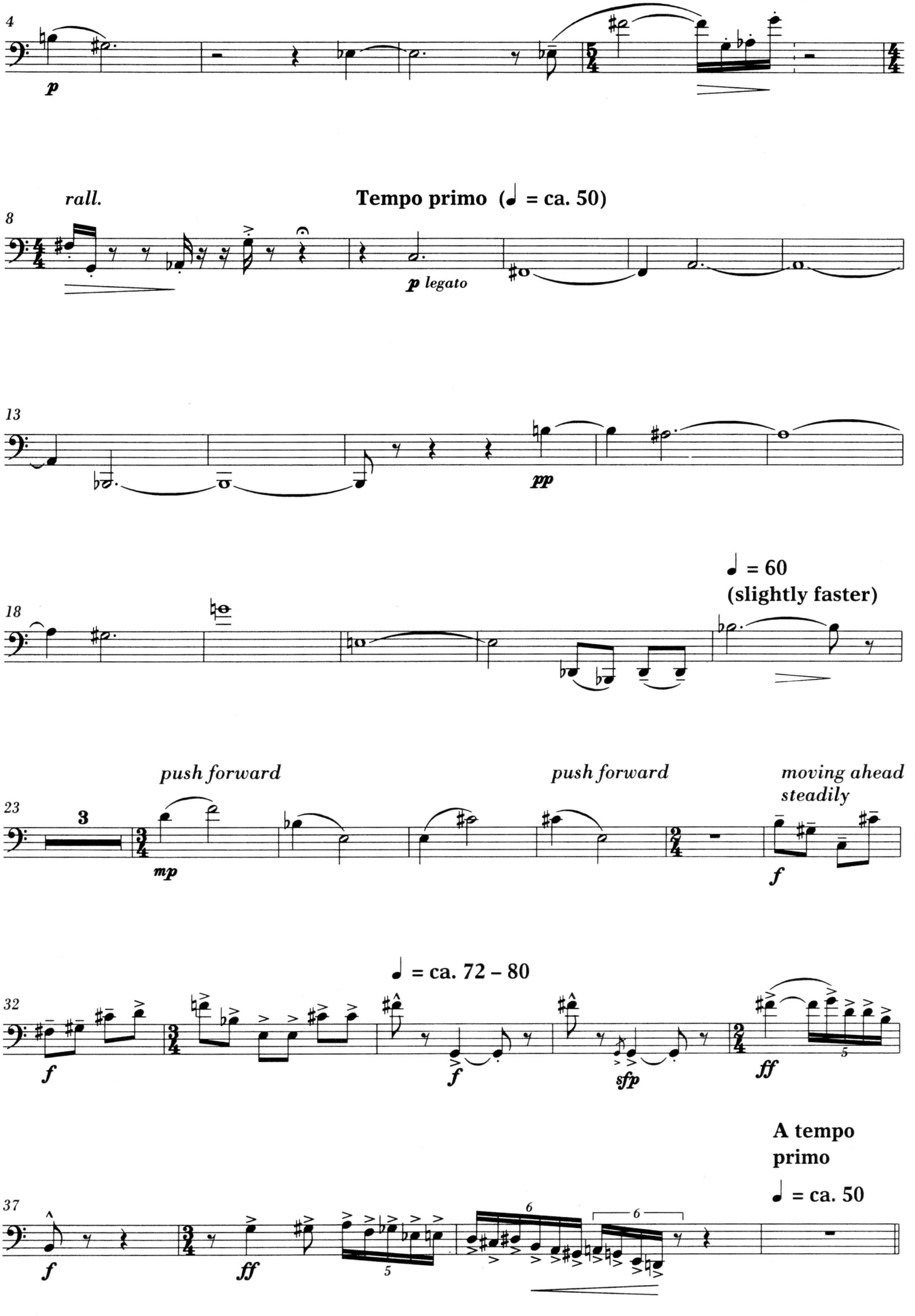
rall.
Tempo primo (♩ = ca. 50)
p legato
♩ = 60
(slightly faster)
push forward
push forward
moving ahead
steadily
♩ = ca. 72 – 80
A tempo
primo
♩ = ca. 50

* *p*, *stacc. ad lib.* with large spaces between the notes (or note groups). Do not coordinate with others. *Slowly cresc.* and *accel.* after all are playing. As tempo becomes faster, *very gradually* line up with other players and make all notes even, so that at the end, all four players are synchronized.

4
p
rall.
Tempo primo (♩ = ca. 50)
8
p legato
13
pp
♩ = 60
(slightly faster)
18
push forward
push forward
moving ahead
steadily
23
3
mp
f
♩ = ca. 72 – 80
32
f
f
sfp
f
A tempo
primo
♩ = ca. 50
37
ff
ff
5
6
6

* *p*, *stacc. ad lib.* with large spaces between the notes (or note groups). Do not coordinate with others. *Slowly cresc.* and *accel.* after all are playing. As tempo becomes faster, *very gradually* line up with other players and make all notes even, so that at the end, all four players are synchronized.

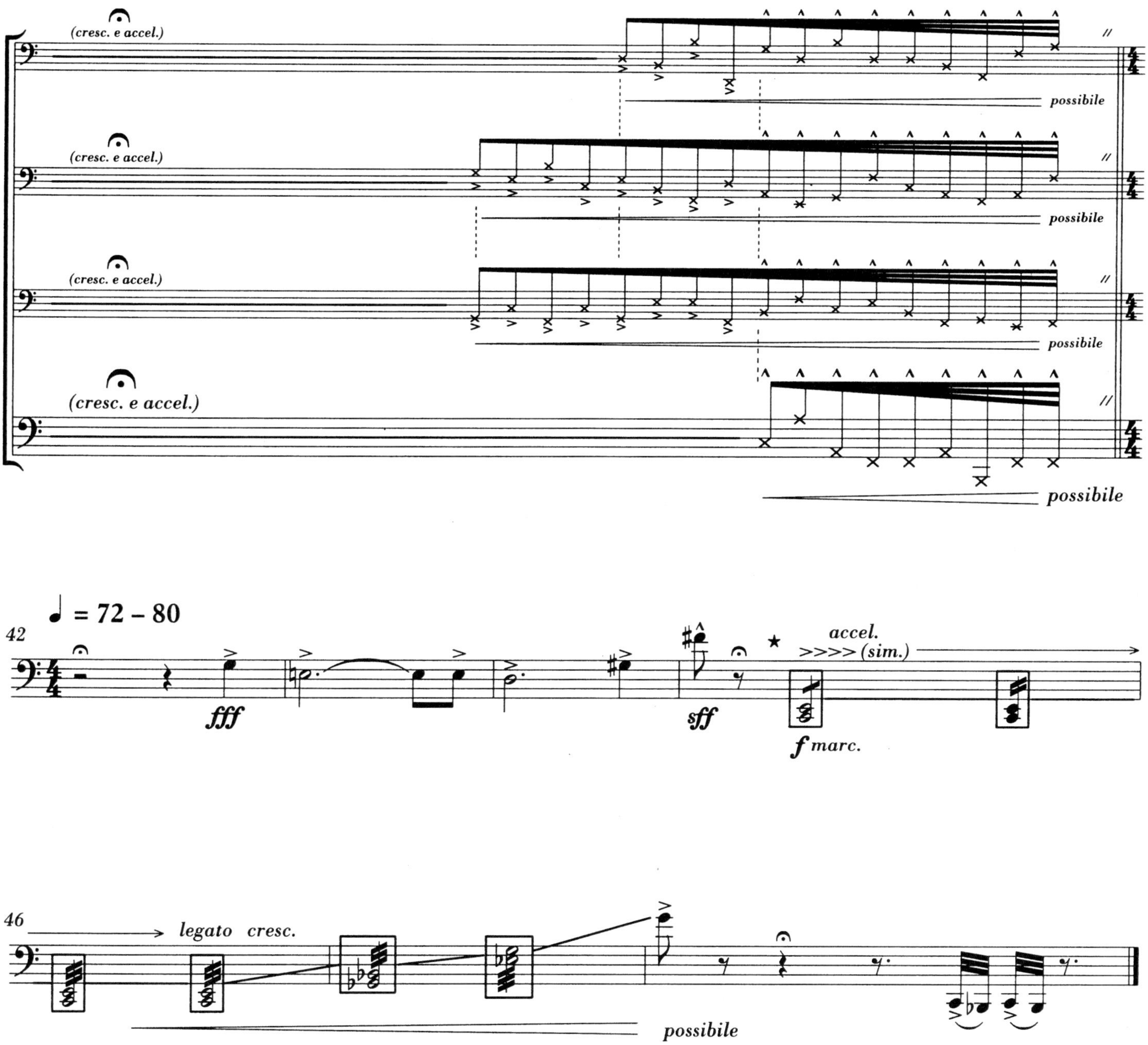

* Play random *ad lib.* constantly changing patterns within, and including, the pitches in the box (5 half-steps). Move upwards to new box gradually where indicated. *Do not* synchronize with other players.

for WNYC

"HOW LIKE PELLUCID STATUES, DADDY OR LIKE A… AN ENGINE."

from *No Longer Very Clear*, by John Ashbery

John Corigliano
(1994)

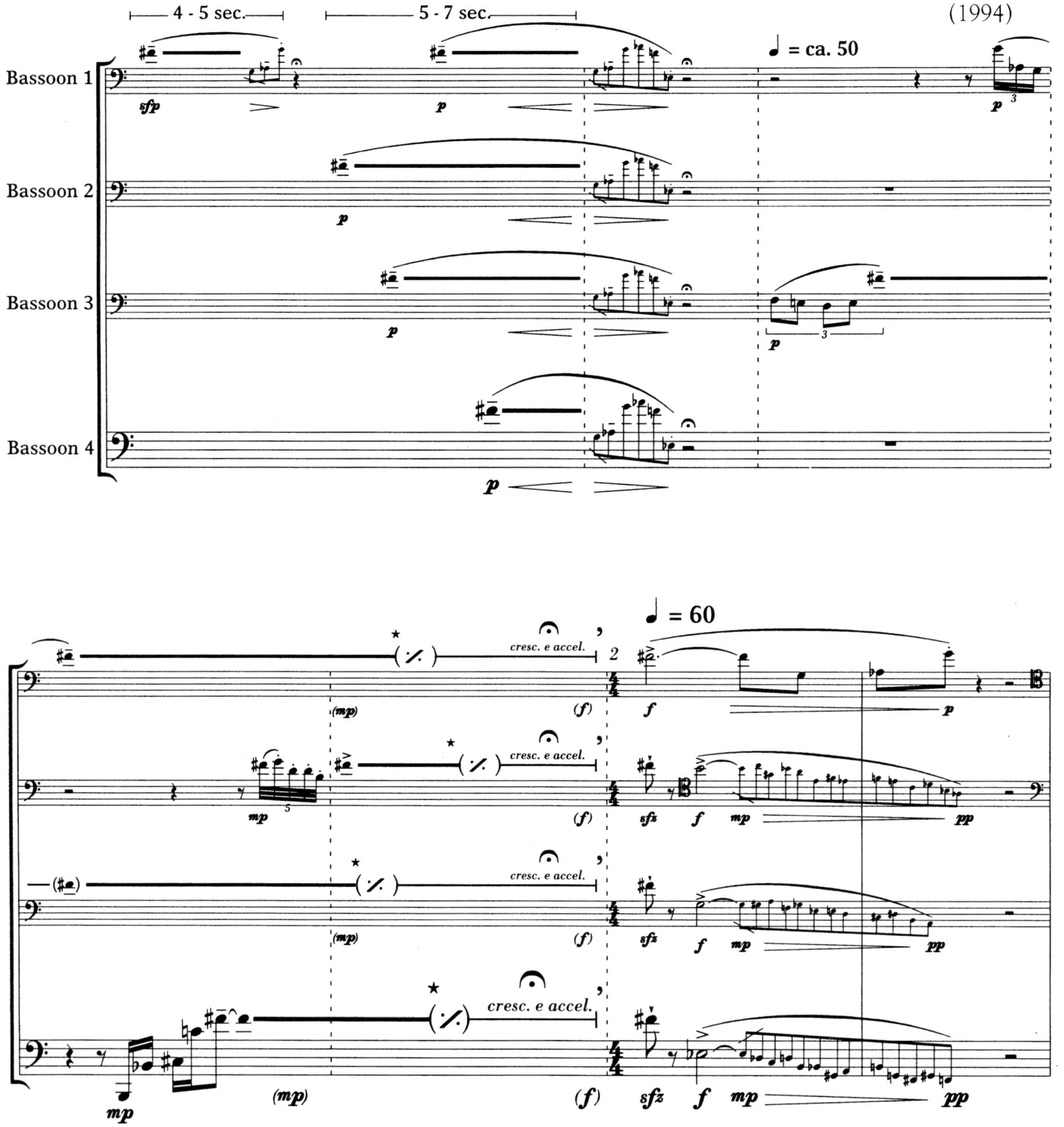

*Repeat figures *ad lib.;* slowly shorten time between figures.

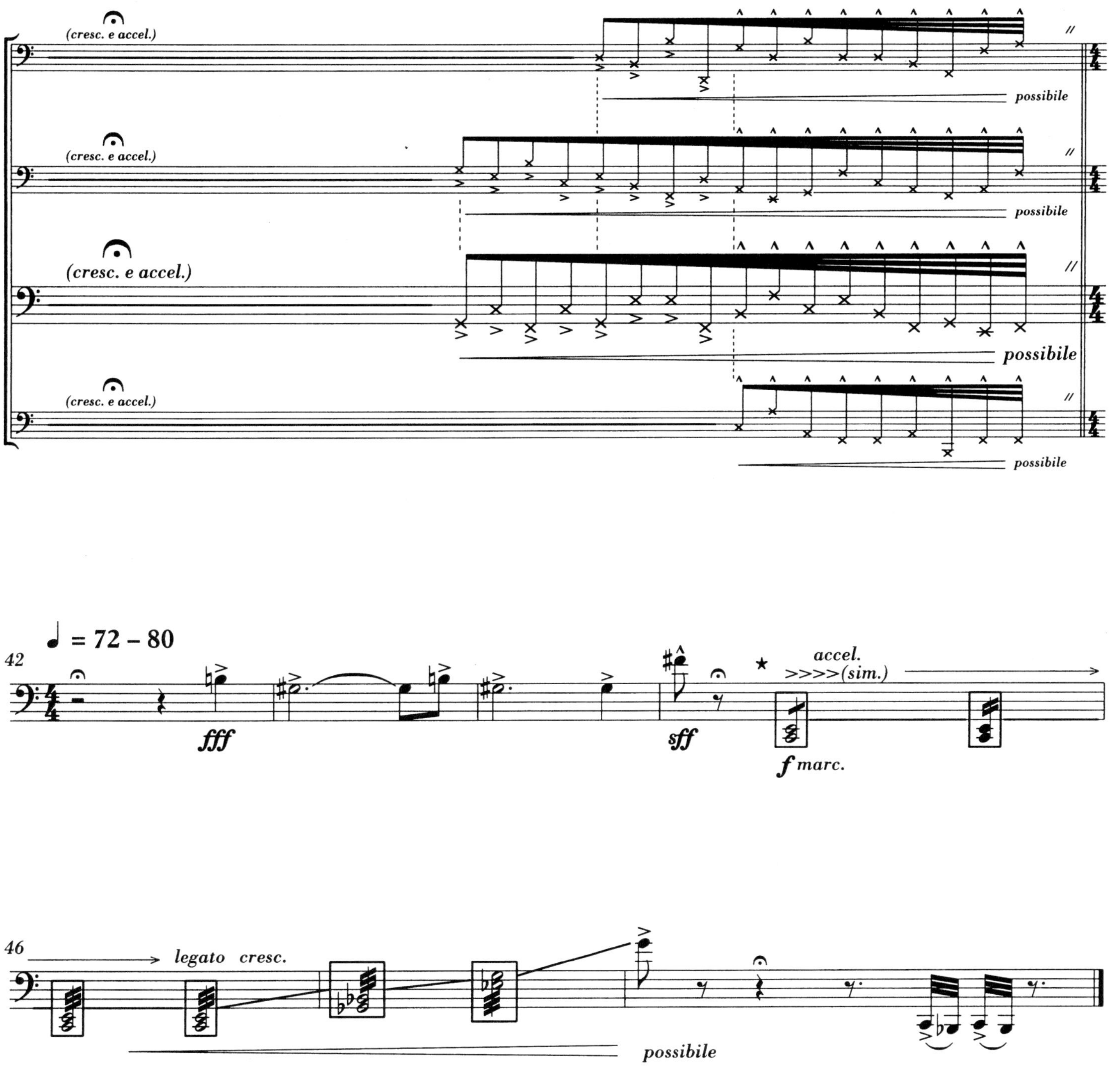

* Play random *ad lib.* constantly changing patterns within, and including, the pitches in the box (5 half-steps). Move upwards to new box gradually where indicated. *Do not* synchronize with other players.

Bassoon 3

for WNYC

"HOW LIKE PELLUCID STATUES, DADDY OR LIKE A… AN ENGINE."

from *No Longer Very Clear*, by John Ashbery

John Corigliano
(1994)

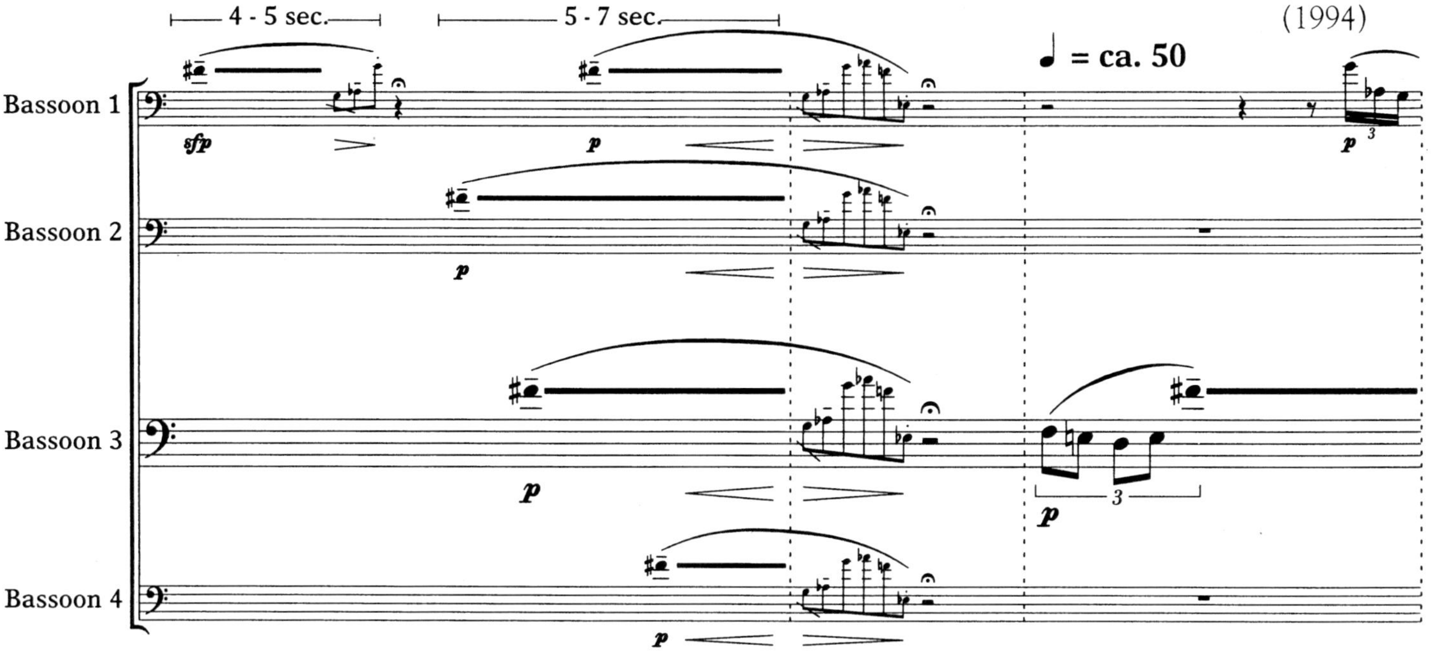

*Repeat figures *ad lib.*; slowly shorten time between figures.

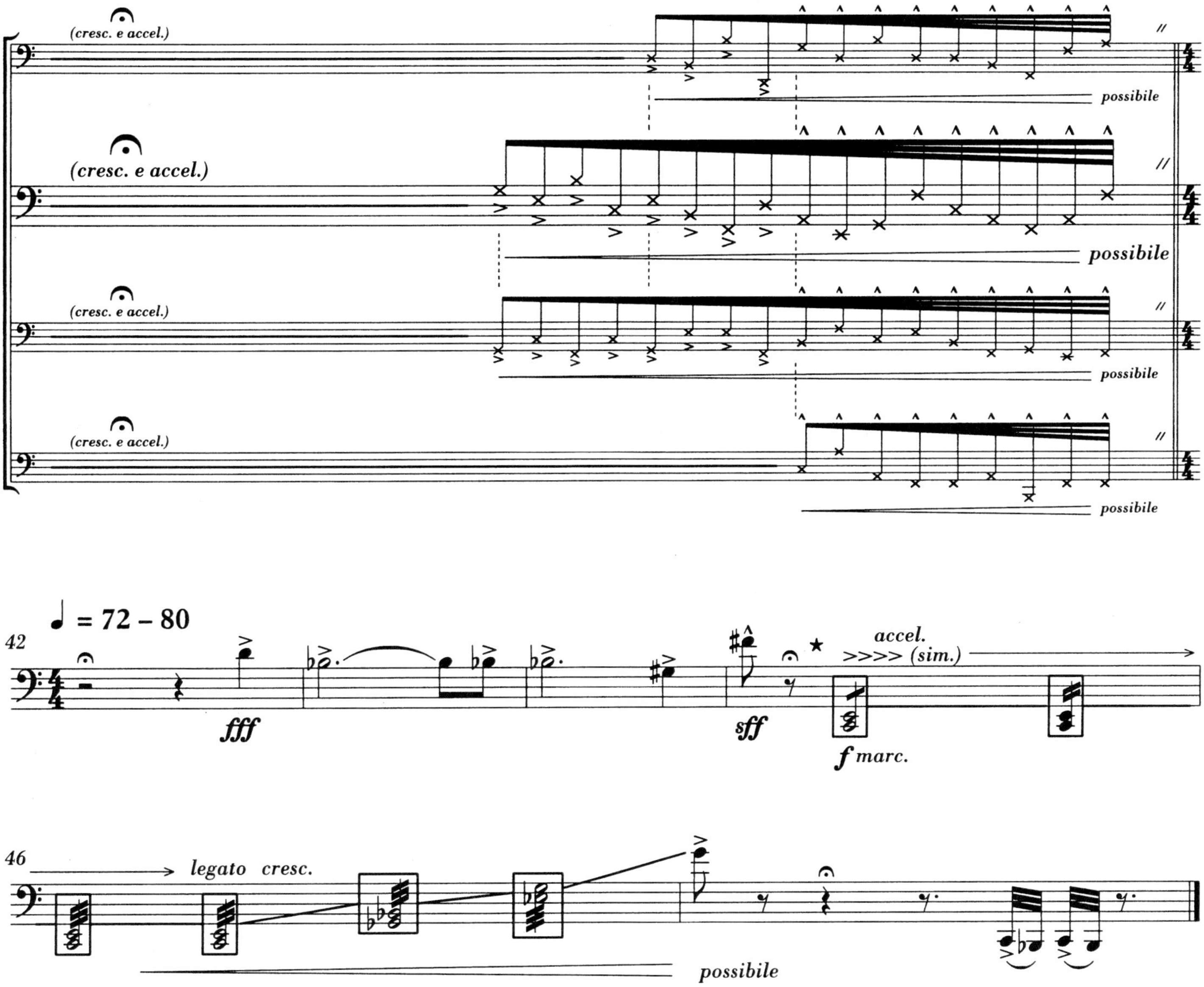

* Play random *ad lib.* constantly changing patterns within, and including, the pitches in the box (5 half-steps). Move upwards to new box gradually where indicated. *Do not* synchronize with other players.

Bassoon 2

for WNYC

"HOW LIKE PELLUCID STATUES, DADDY OR LIKE A... AN ENGINE."

from *No Longer Very Clear*, by John Ashbery

John Corigliano
(1994)

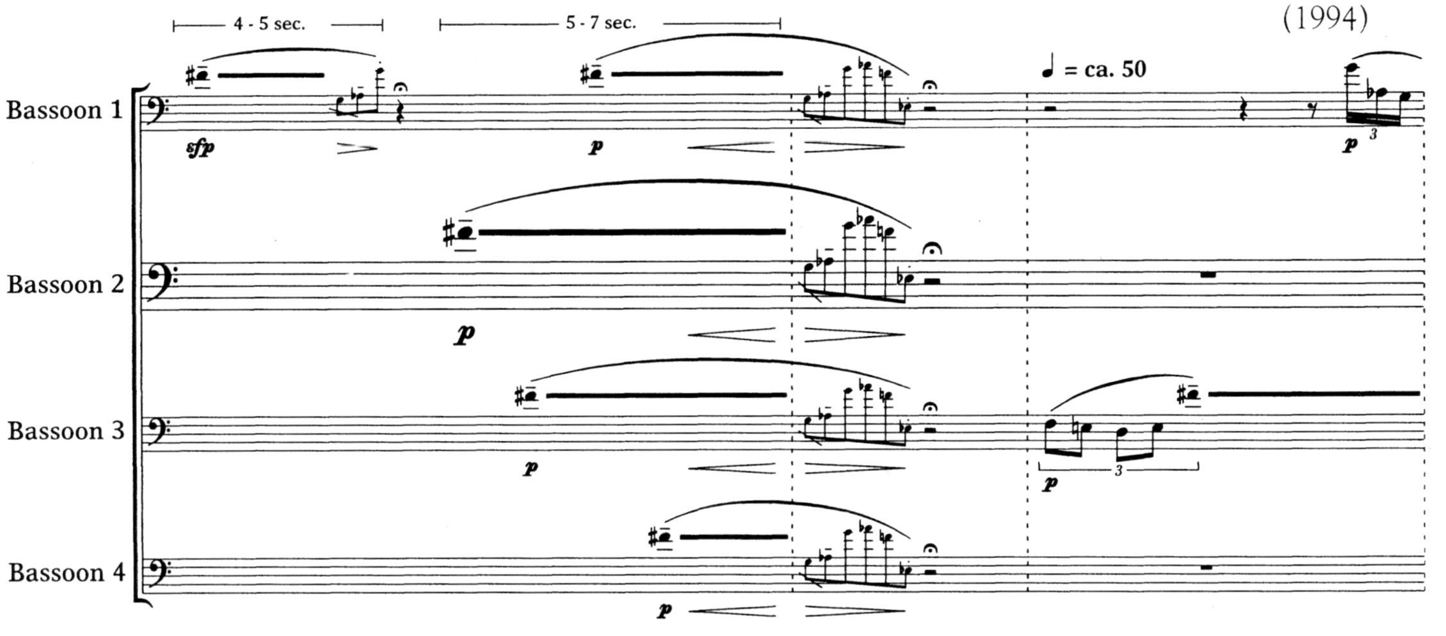

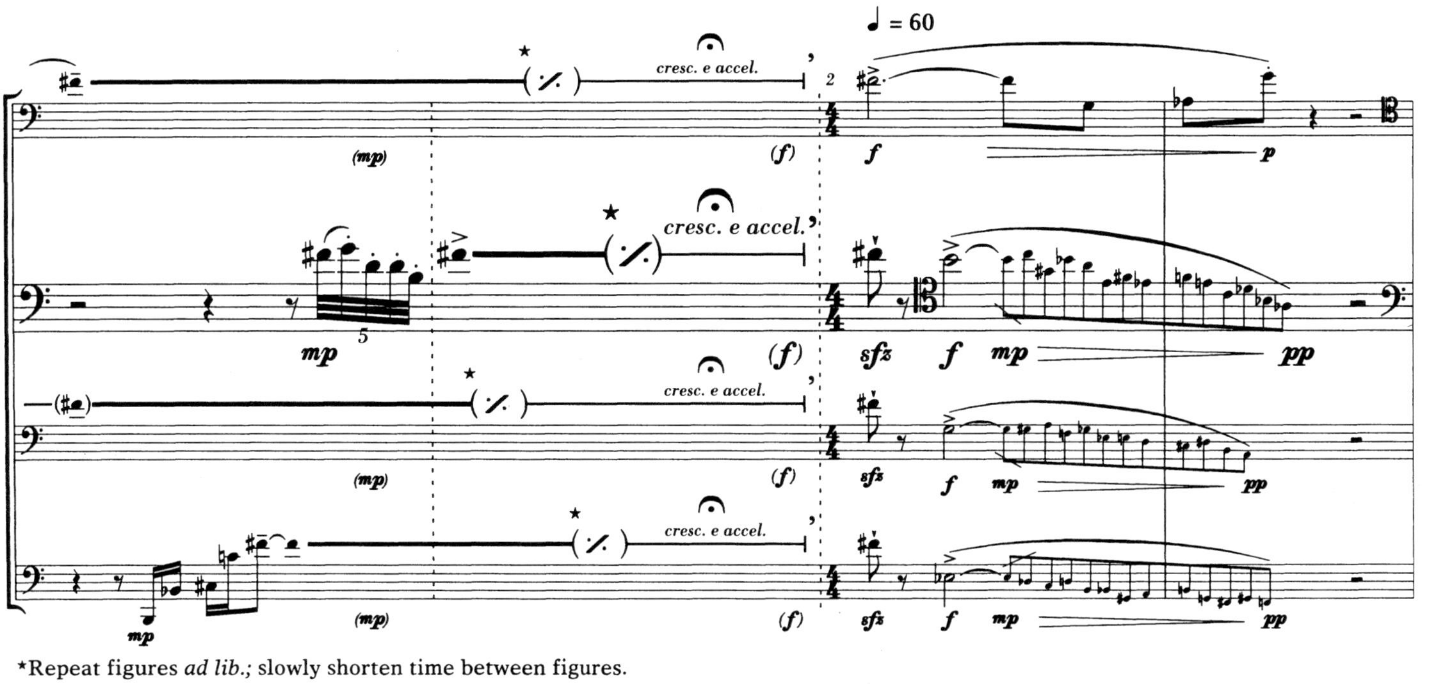

*Repeat figures *ad lib.;* slowly shorten time between figures.

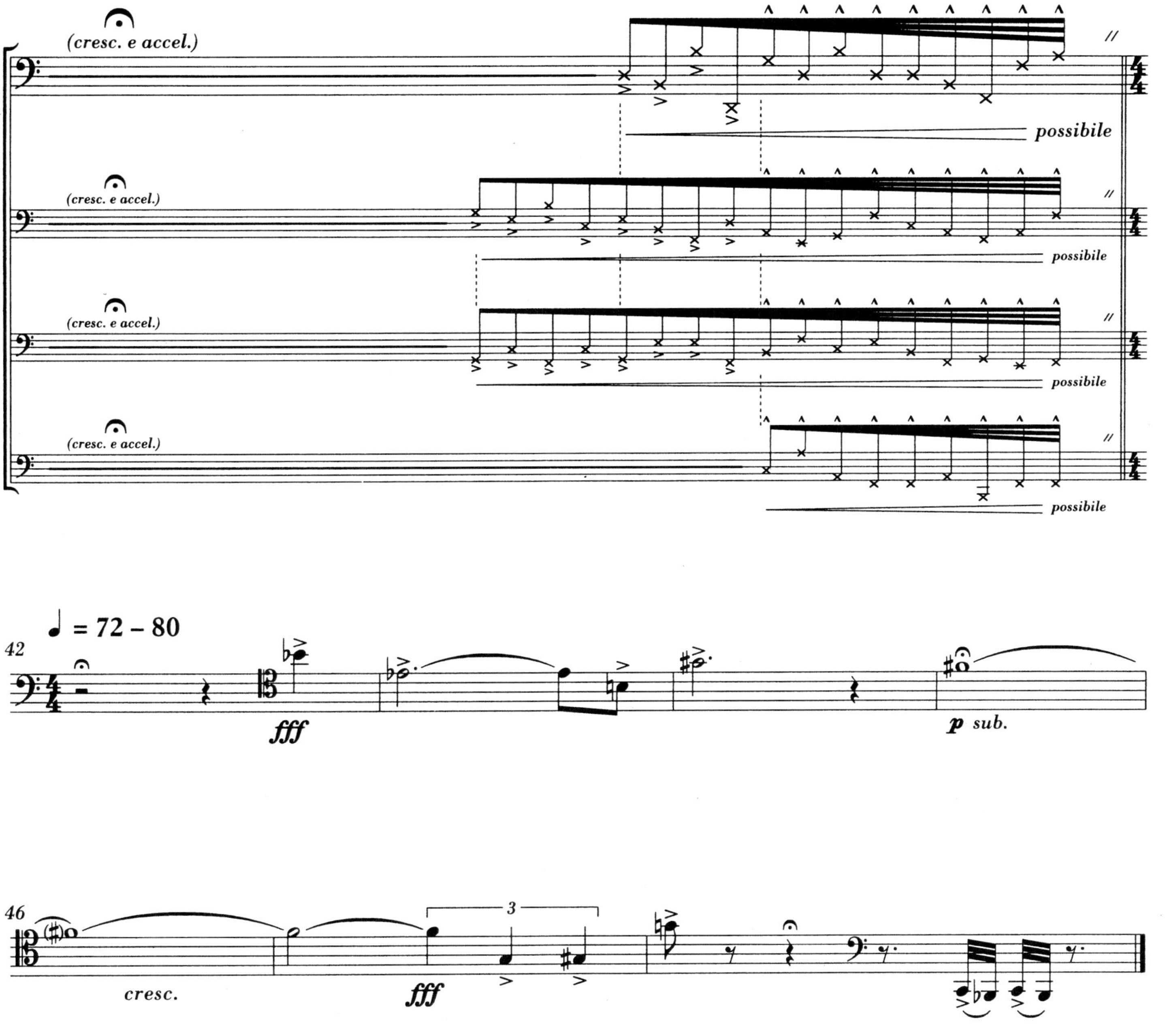
(cresc. e accel.)
possibile
(cresc. e accel.)
possibile
(cresc. e accel.)
possibile
(cresc. e accel.)
possibile
♩ = 72 – 80
42
fff
p sub.
46
cresc.
3
fff

Bassoon 1

for WNYC

"HOW LIKE PELLUCID STATUES, DADDY OR LIKE A… AN ENGINE."

from *No Longer Very Clear*, by John Ashbery

John Corigliano
(1994)

★Repeat figures *ad lib.;* slowly shorten time between figures.

push forward
moving ahead steadily
27
= ca. 72 – 80
33
A tempo primo
= ca. 50
37

* *p, stacc. ad lib.* with large spaces between the notes (or note groups). Do not coordinate with others. *Slowly cresc.* and *accel.* after all are playing. As tempo becomes faster, *very gradually* line up with other players and make all notes even, so that at the end, all four players are synchronized.

* Play random *ad lib.* constantly changing patterns within, and including, the pitches in the box (5 half-steps). Move upwards to new box gradually where indicated. *Do not* synchronize with other players.